I Wish I Were a Humpback Whale

by Christina Jordan

Illustrated by Gabhor Utomo

magic wagon

visit us at www.abdopublishing.com

For Ryan, my ocean boy. —CJ

Published by Magic Wagon, a division of the ABDO Group, 8000 West 78th Street, Edina, Minnesota 55439. Copyright © 2012 by Abdo Consulting Group, Inc. International copyrights reserved in all countries. All rights reserved. No part of this book may be reproduced in any form without written permission from the publisher.

Looking Glass Library™ is a trademark and logo of Magic Wagon.

Printed in the United States of America, North Mankato, Minnesota.
042011
092011
 This book contains at least 10% recycled materials.

Written by Christina Jordan
Illustrations by Gabhor Utomo
Edited by Stephanie Hedlund and Rochelle Baltzer
Cover and interior layout and design by Abbey Fitzgerald

About the Author: Christina Jordan has been an elementary school teacher for 20 years. She also holds a MA in Psychology, is a wife and a mother of three children. Combining her passion for her profession, education, and her family inspired her to add "author" to her list of accomplishments. The "I Wish I Were . . ." books are Ms. Jordan's first series of children's books.

About the Illustrator: Gabhor Utomo was born in Indonesia, studied art in San Francisco, and worked as an illustrator since he graduated in 2003. He has illustrated a number of children's books and has won several awards from local and national art organizations. He spends his spare time running around the house with his wife and twin daughters.

Library of Congress Cataloging-in-Publication Data

Jordan, Christina.
  I wish I were a humpback whale / by Christina Jordan ; illustrated by Gabhor Utomo.
     p. cm. -- (I wish I were--)
  Summary: A young boy imagines how different his life would be if he were a humpback whale.
  ISBN 978-1-61641-658-4
  [1. Stories in rhyme. 2. Humpback whale--Fiction. 3. Whales--Fiction.] I. Utomo, Gabhor, ill. II. Title.
  PZ8.3.J7646Iaq 2011
  [E]--dc22
                                                    2010048716

I wish I were a humpback whale swimming in the sea.
Life would be much easier than it is being me.

3

My home would be the big, wide space of the ocean blue.
Out there I'd have no screaming sisters (mine are five and two!).

With ocean friends I'd swim and dive. And we would have such fun!
We wouldn't have to clean up all our toys when we were done.

6

There'd be no need to waste my time making up my bed.
I'd use my time to splash my tail on great big waves instead.

I'd have no rules like "be polite," "sit still," and "always share." Instead I'd spend my time breaching waves without a care.

When I'd sing my high-pitched song, as humpbacks often do,
I'd make it loud enough to reach everyone I knew.

No one would ever say to me, "You can't. You're just too small."
'Cause as a humpback whale I'd be one of the biggest creatures of all!

15

But, if I were a humpback whale there would be things I'd miss. Like hiking to the creek with Dad to play and catch some fish.

16

Chocolate milk and ice cream cones could no longer be my treats.
Plankton and some tiny fish is all I'd get to eat.

And if the many ocean sounds ever gave me a fright,
there'd be no one to read me books and tuck me in at night.

21

Oh, humpback whale, it would be such fun to live with you in the sea. But right now I like my life. I think I'll just stay me!

23

A "Ton" of Cool Facts about Whales

- Although they live in water, whales are not fish. They are mammals.

- Humpback whales do not have teeth. They take in food through baleen, a series of 250 flexible plates that filter water and food.

- Despite eating only small plants and fish, humpback whales grow to be up to 48 feet (15 m) long. That's the size of a bus! They weigh up to 40 tons (36 T)!

- Whales travel in groups called pods.

- Male humpback whales sing beautiful songs that can travel for miles throughout the ocean. Each song lasts from 20 minutes up to several hours. Scientists believe they sing to communicate with other humpbacks.

Glossary

breach - to jump or leap out of the water.

plankton - small animals and plants that float in a body of water.

polite - showing good manners by the way you act or speak.

Web Sites

To learn more about humpback whales, visit ABDO Group online at **www.abdopublishing.com**. Web sites about humpback whales are featured on our Book Links page. These links are routinely monitored and updated to provide the most current information available.